THE MYSTERY OF THE TIGER'S EYE

created by
GERTRUDE CHANDLER WARNER

Illustrated by Hodges Soileau

SCHOLASTIC INC.
New York Toronto London Auckland Sydney
New Delhi Mexico City Hong Kong Buenos Aires

Activities by Kimberly Weinberger
Activity Illustrations by Alfred Giuliani

ISBN 0-439-24099-9

12 11 10 9 8 7 6 5 4 3   1 2 3 4 5 6/0

Printed in the U.S.A.   40
First Scholastic printing, October 2001

Contents

CHAPTER 1

A Very Unusual House

Ten-year-old Violet Alden gazed out the window of Grandfather's new minivan. The gray-green water of the Chesapeake Bay sparkled in the autumn sun.

"Everything looks golden here," Violet remarked. She was an artist and always noticed the scenery.

"The sun is low in the fall," said her fourteen-year-old brother, Henry. "Also, Maryland is a lot farther south than Connecticut."

Next to him, Jessie Alden nodded. "It was

cold when we left Greenfield. I hope we packed the right clothes."

Even though she was only twelve, Jessie liked to take care of her brothers and sister.

"Grandfather, tell us about your friend again," Benny said. At six, he was the youngest of the four children.

"Edward Singleton and I were college roommates," James Alden replied. "Edward used to take me to fairs and carnivals. He loved to ride the rides and play games."

"So do I," said Benny. He was going to like Grandfather's friend.

"We've been in touch over the years," said Grandfather. "When we finished school, he moved to Maryland and started collecting things from carnivals and state fairs. It became his life's work."

"What kinds of things?" Jessie inquired. Collecting sounded like a strange job to her.

"He'll show us when we get to Cliffwalk Manor," said Grandfather. "I hear he has a most unusual house. Maybe a little *too* unusual."

Violet turned away from the window. "What do you mean?"

"When Edward called me, he was very upset," said Grandfather. "He asked me to come to Heron's Bay because of some strange happenings in his house."

"Sounds like a mystery," Violet said eagerly.

Benny bounced in his seat. "Oh, boy! A new mystery!"

Grandfather smiled. "People must know that you kids are pretty good detectives."

"We *have* cracked lots of cases," Henry agreed.

"I think we solve cases because there are four of us," Jessie added. "Four heads are better than one."

"I only have one head," Benny chimed in.

Everyone laughed.

Jessie ruffled Benny's hair. "That's an expression. It means we figure out things together."

The Alden children had always stuck together. When their parents died, the children had moved into an abandoned boxcar. Eventually their grandfather found them and they went to live in his big house in Greenfield. Now they traveled all over the country and had adventures.

The minivan began climbing a steep road.

"Cliffwalk Manor is up here," said Grandfather.

When they drove into a clearing at the top of the bluff, they all gasped.

Cliffwalk Manor was an enormous mansion of brownstone, granite, and wood. Two round towers flanked a huge stained-glass window over the front door. The house seemed gloomy, even in the sun.

The kids tumbled out onto the gravel driveway.

A white-haired gentleman came down the steps to greet them. He had blue eyes and a short white beard.

"James!" he exclaimed. "Thank you for coming."

Grandfather clasped his friend's hand. "Edward, it's been too long. These are my

grandchildren, Henry, Jessie, Violet, and Benny."

"Welcome to Cliffwalk Manor," said Mr. Singleton. "Your grandfather has told me a great deal about you. Please come inside."

They walked into an echoing entryway. Light from the stained-glass window made colorful patterns on the marble floor. A large carved cabinet covered the opposite wall.

"What a big house," Violet commented.

"Cliffwalk Manor has been in my family for generations," Edward said proudly. "My grandfather, Captain Singleton, had a small fleet of oyster boats. He built this place around the turn of the century."

They went into the dining room.

Benny's eyes lit up. "Wow! A real merry-go-round horse sticking up in the middle of the table!"

Edward laughed. "The chariot seats around the table are from the same merry-go-round."

Benny couldn't wait to sit in a red-and-green-painted dragon chariot. "I hope we eat soon!"

Jessie discovered a mechanical fortune-teller behind a glass-beaded curtain. Edward gave her a brass token to put in the slot. The figure whirred to life, cackling and waving over her crystal ball. Then a brown-edged, yellowed card dropped in the brass tray.

"What's your fortune?" asked Grandfather.

"It says, 'You will take many trips,' " Jessie read. "Well, that's certainly true!"

"Madame ZaZa is about eighty years old," Edward said. "Her fortunes are still accurate today."

"Boy, you have a lot of stuff!" Benny remarked as their host led them through rooms filled with glass display cases.

"As your grandfather probably told you, I collect things from carnivals and fairs," said Edward. "I'll give you a better tour later. I'm sure you're tired after that drive."

"We're fine," said Grandfather. "We'd really like to know what is bothering you."

"Let's go in the parlor, where we can be

comfortable," said Edward. "It's a rather long story."

They went into a huge room with high ceilings decorated in gold leaf. The old-fashioned furniture had curvy legs and burgundy velvet cushions.

When everyone was seated, Edward continued. "One night, many, many years ago, my grandfather hosted a party," he said. "A lot of rich society people came. Two brothers who performed a magic act were hired for entertainment. I suppose the crowd was more interested in eating and talking than watching a couple of men do card tricks. The youngest magician became angry because they weren't paying attention."

"What did he do?" asked Jessie.

"He announced to the party-goers they would be sorry they'd ignored him," Edward replied. "He said he would be a great performer one day and astound audiences the world over." Edward's voice dropped to a hush. "Then the young man predicted odd things would happen in this very building. He would leave something of himself behind."

Violet's eyes were wide. "Did anyone find anything?"

Edward shook his head. "No one found anything unusual. At least, not that I know of. But some very strange things began happening about a month ago."

"What kind of things?" Henry asked.

"Pictures shifting from one room to another on different floors," Edward replied. "Books falling out of bookcases when no one was around. The clock stops and starts at odd times. One morning I found a playing card in the kitchen sink! Nobody in this house plays cards."

Henry leaned forward, interested. "Who were the magicians at that party?"

"They were called the Houdini Brothers. One of the brothers was Harry Houdini," said Edward.

Henry was impressed. "Harry Houdini was the most famous magician in the world! He was an escape artist. He'd be locked in a trunk with chains around his hands and feet and he'd still get out."

"Cool!" Benny said. "And he was here?"

"Yes, but I think Harry Houdini was simply showing off that night," Edward stated. "He was very young, just starting out as a performer."

Grandfather looked seriously at his friend. "Are these strange events still going on?"

Edward nodded with dismay. "James, it's very important to stop these . . . pranks. I want Cliffwalk Manor to be a nice place for my great-nephew."

Grandfather lifted his eyebrows. "Your great-nephew is here? I thought he lived in Europe."

At that moment, footsteps clomped down the grand staircase. The sullen face of a dark-haired boy around Jessie's age appeared in the doorway.

"Oh," he said. "I see these people are here."

"Come in, Dorsey," said Edward. "Meet James Alden, my college roommate. And these are his grandchildren — Henry, Jessie, Violet, and Benny. Everyone, this is my great-nephew, Dorsey Pindar."

The Aldens said hello, but Dorsey merely scowled.

"When is dinner?" he demanded. "I'm starving."

"In a little while," replied his great-uncle. "The Aldens need to get settled first."

"Hurry up," Dorsey said. "I'm used to eating at exactly six o'clock." He stomped back up the marble stairs.

Edward turned an apologetic face toward his guests. "Please excuse my great-nephew. I'm afraid he's had a different lifestyle. His parents — my niece and her husband — are archaeologists. They are on a dig in North Africa for the next two years."

"Dorsey doesn't live with them?" asked Grandfather.

"No, he's always gone to boarding schools in either England or Europe," replied Edward. "But now my niece and her husband have decided that he should be in the States. So they found a boarding school in Virginia. He's only staying with me until the school starts next week."

"It must be hard for a young boy to live with strangers," Grandfather said sympathetically.

"We wouldn't want to live with anyone but you, Grandfather," Violet said loyally.

Edward sighed. "I've been trying to convince Suzanne, my niece, that Dorsey should stay with me. He doesn't know me very well, but at least I'm a relative. He can go to school in Heron's Bay. But it doesn't seem as if he wants to live here. With everything that's been happening, I can see why."

"Would you like us to help find out what is going on?" Grandfather offered. "My grandchildren are very good at solving mysteries."

"Will you help me?" Edward asked the Alden children. "Dorsey leaves for boarding school on Sunday."

Henry spoke for them all. "We'll do our best."

"Good! I'll show you to your rooms now."

Edward Singleton led them to spacious rooms on the third floor.

The children stood in the corridor after Grandfather had gone into his room at the end of the hall.

"I still can't believe Harry Houdini was here," Henry said.

"I think he's still here," said Benny.

Jessie looked at him. "What do you mean?"

"Who else do you think is doing all this stuff?" Benny whispered. "It has to be the ghost of Harry Houdini!"

CHAPTER 2

The Figure on the Stairs

That evening Edward cooked a special dinner. Before the meal, everyone enjoyed crab puffs and tiny pizzas on the back deck.

"What a great view," Henry commented, leaning on the rail.

Pleasure boats and Coast Guard cutters dotted the dark blue waters of the bay. A flock of geese flew over in a long V, heading south for the winter.

"Feel free to use the telescope." Edward

indicated the telescope mounted on one side of the deck railing. He went back inside the house to check on dinner.

Benny hopped up on the stool and peered through the eyepiece. "I see land!"

"That's the eastern shore," spoke a new voice. "Heron's Bay is located on the western shore of the Chesapeake Bay."

The children turned to see a tall woman around the same age as Grandfather and Edward Singleton. She wore a flowing purple silk caftan and a matching fringed scarf tied around her silvery curls. Blue and purple beads swung around her neck. She smiled at the children.

"Hello," she said. "I'm Iona Levitt, Edward's friend."

"Pleased to meet you," said Grandfather, walking over to shake her hand. "I'm James Alden. And these are my grandchildren."

The Aldens greeted Iona each in turn.

"How lucky you are to have such fine grandchildren," Iona said to Grandfather. "I never married, so I don't have any."

Edward came through the French doors with a tray of drinks and more crab puffs, hot from the oven.

"Iona owns the gift shop in Heron's Bay," he commented. "We'll visit when we go into town. I hope you brought your wonderful pecan pie," he said to her.

She grinned at him. "I knew you'd need dessert. So I brought two pecan pies, your favorite." When Edward left once more, she said, "He's so busy with those collections, sometimes he forgets to eat. I close my shop at four and often come here to fix dinner for him."

"Are you a good cook?" Benny asked. "As good as Mr. Singleton?" He had eaten six crab puffs already.

Iona laughed heartily. "I bet you like to eat!"

"It's my favorite thing in the world," Benny told her.

Everyone laughed.

Just then another guest stepped onto the deck.

"Hi," she said shyly. "You must be the Aldens. I'm Melanie Preston."

Melanie was young, around twenty. She wore her light brown hair in a long braid. Pale green eyes peered owlishly from behind large-framed glasses.

Edward came out behind her. "I see you've met Melanie. She goes to college here. She's taking a break this semester to catalog my collections. Melanie knows more about what I have than I do!"

"It's been a wonderful opportunity," Melanie said in her whispery voice. "I'm very lucky."

"She works until evening, so she usually eats with us, too," said Edward. He glanced around. "Dorsey isn't here. Would you call him down, Melanie? It's nearly time to eat."

Melanie went back into the house. When she returned, a surly-looking Dorsey was on her heels.

"How come you didn't tell me it was a party?" he said accusingly to Edward. "All the good stuff is gone."

"I told you this morning we were having appetizers on the deck before dinner," Edward answered. "Then I called you again, but your door was shut. I guess you didn't hear me."

"Nobody pays attention to me," Dorsey complained. "I'll be glad to go to that school next week."

Edward exchanged a glance with Iona and shook his head slightly.

They all went into the dining room and took their seats in the chariots around the big table with the merry-go-round horse in the center.

Each place was set with colorful china. Beside every dinner fork was a small favor, a souvenir from the 1893 Chicago World's Fair.

Benny got a set of dominoes. Henry received a silver pen shaped like a feather. Violet's gift was a glass shoe with a pincushion. Jessie got a small fan, and Grandfather received a miniature cast-iron Ferris wheel.

"These are wonderful," Grandfather exclaimed, setting the wheel spinning. "But aren't they valuable?"

"Duplicates," Edward said. "I don't need

more than one of each, so I'm delighted to give these away."

Iona, Melanie, and Dorsey had similar presents.

When Edward went into the kitchen, Iona said, "Edward has too much stuff. His collections rule his life."

"I heard that," Edward said, returning with a fragrant-smelling platter of Maryland fried chicken. "Iona thinks I should sell Cliffwalk Manor."

"Well, you should!" she said emphatically. "This place is too big for one person. And you spend too much time fooling with that junk."

Edward put bowls of mashed potatoes and gravy on the table. "That 'junk,' as you call it, is worth a great deal of money," he said.

Dorsey, who had been greedily reaching for the chicken, stopped. "It is?"

"Yes," said his great-uncle. "Think about how long ago the Chicago World's Fair was. Over a hundred years! Many of my things are fragile and hard to find, like souvenir books and tickets."

Dorsey sniffed. "Those things look like grubby pieces of paper to me."

"They may not look like much, but they represent pieces of history," Edward said. "Scholars have asked to study my collections. That's why I'm having this young student get them in order."

"What is your major in college?" James Alden asked Melanie.

She tugged nervously on her long braid. "Uh — I'm just taking some drama classes."

"Do you want to be an actress?" asked Henry.

Melanie's fork clattered to the floor. "Sorry. I guess I'll be an entertainer of some sort."

Iona went into the kitchen to get Melanie a clean fork.

"Excuse me," Melanie said, rising from the swan chariot. "I think I'll skip dinner and go home. I'll see you all early tomorrow."

"She'll miss dessert — that's the best part!" Benny said, amazed anyone would leave a meal before the end.

"I want some more iced tea," Dorsey said. He got up, too, and took his glass into the kitchen.

Jessie was surprised. Dorsey didn't seem like the type to fetch for himself.

Iona came back in with a new fork for Melanie and another plate of chicken. "Melanie's gone? That's funny. She usually loves fried chicken."

"More for the rest of us," said Edward, patting his round stomach.

Half spilling his too-full glass of tea, Dorsey slid into the swan chariot he had been sharing with Melanie.

"Me first," he demanded, watching Iona serve the chicken.

"Guests first," Edward gently admonished.

The corners of Dorsey's mouth turned down and he rapped the table impatiently with his fork.

Before Edward could correct his great-nephew's behavior, a wheezing sound started up behind the beaded curtain.

The mechanical fortune-teller was moving! Cackling, she nodded and waved her gnarled fingers over the crystal ball.

Edward frowned. "Who dropped a token in Madame ZaZa?"

"Not me," Dorsey said quickly.

"Well, it wasn't any of us," said Edward. "We've been sitting here the whole time. Only you, Iona, and Melanie got up from the table. And Melanie has gone for the day."

"Maybe somebody accidentally bumped Madame ZaZa," Iona said smoothly. "It's a mechanical device, Edward. And a very old one at that."

"She only works if you drop in a token," Edward insisted. "Someone made her start up."

Someone, thought Violet. *Or something.*

"This is the kind of thing I'm talking about," Edward said to Grandfather. "Somebody is making these things happen. But I don't know who. Or why."

"Look." Benny drew a yellowed card from the fortune-teller's brass tray. "Here's the little card. What does it say, Violet?" He was still learning to read.

Violet squinted at the faded printing. "It says, 'You are in for a big change.' "

"Who?" Benny wanted to know. "Who is in for a big change?"

"Maybe Edward is," Iona said with a coy smile.

"What kind of change?" Benny pressed.

Grandfather stood. "It's getting late, kids. We all need to get to bed."

The children went upstairs to their rooms. Dorsey went with them.

His room was across the hall from the bedroom Jessie and Violet were sharing. A large trunk stood outside the door.

"Stupid trunk," he said gloomily. "All I ever do is pack and unpack my stuff."

Benny tapped the hollow trunk. "If you stayed here, you wouldn't have to pack."

Dorsey stared at him. "Are you nuts? Stay in this weird house?" Without another word, he went into his room and shut the door.

Before the door closed completely, Violet caught a glimpse of something on the floor of his room. It looked like a metal box with wires coming out of it.

What is that? she wondered. *Some kind of an invention?*

Before she could mention it, Benny said, "I wonder what's wrong with Dorsey. I like this house!"

"Maybe he's homesick," Jessie suggested.

Henry nodded. "He might miss his parents."

Jessie and Violet said good night, then went into their own room. It was very nice, with rose-covered wallpaper and two canopy beds.

Violet was almost asleep when she heard something overhead.

Thump, thump. Scrape, thump.

She sat up. "What was that?"

"I don't know." Jessie had heard it, too. "Sounded like somebody moving furniture."

"Who'd be moving furniture this time of night?" Violet threw back the covers and slipped into her bathrobe. "I think we'd better check it out."

Dorsey Pindar was standing in the hall.

"Did you hear the noises, too?" Jessie asked him.

"Yeah," he said. "Sounds like somebody is in the attic."

"We're going to see," Violet told him.

"I'll show you the attic door." Dorsey went ahead of them.

Down the hall, they met Benny and Henry coming out of their room.

"We heard something," Benny reported.

"So did we. We're going up into the attic to see what it is," Jessie said.

Dorsey opened a white-painted door at the end of the hall. He yanked a string that turned on a dim lightbulb. Stairs led steeply upward, cloaked in shadows.

Jessie went first. Her bare feet made no sound on the wooden steps.

On the landing, she stopped, then gasped. She was not alone!

A face with huge, dark eyes stared back at her.

CHAPTER 3

The Magician Returns

Jessie stepped back, startled. Then she realized she was looking at her own reflection!

"It's a mirror!" she exclaimed.

But not an ordinary mirror. The tall, wood-framed mirror had curved glass. The uneven surface made her eyes seem large and her face look ghostly.

Dorsey moved in front of Jessie. His reflection wavered like a ghost, too.

"It's a fun-house mirror," he said. "But it doesn't belong here. The mirror is supposed to be at the end of the landing."

"Somebody moved it," Violet said. "That must be what we heard."

"Who would shove a heavy mirror in the middle of the night?" Henry wondered aloud.

"I'm not sticking around to find out!" said Dorsey. "This house is just too weird!"

He almost ran back down the stairs.

"Do you think it's a ghost?" Benny asked. The attic landing *was* creepy in the dim light. Shadows seemed to leap out at them.

"Let's investigate in the morning," Jessie decided. She wasn't exactly afraid, but something about the attic made her nervous.

"Good idea," Henry agreed. "Let's go back to bed, everybody."

Snuggled under the covers once more, Jessie realized why she had felt uneasy on the attic steps. It wasn't just *who* moved the fun-house mirror, but *why*?

Was someone trying to scare the Aldens off from solving this mystery?

*   *   *

Sunshine poured through the wide windows in a golden stream, waking Jessie. The notion of ghosts in the attic seemed silly on such a cheerful autumn day.

Violet was already up and dressed. "Better hurry for breakfast, sleepyhead."

Jessie quickly pulled on jeans and a sweatshirt. The girls met their brothers in the hall.

"I'm starving!" Benny declared.

"When *aren't* you starving?" Violet said with a laugh.

Downstairs, breakfast was set out on the sideboard in the dining room.

Edward and Grandfather were drinking coffee on the deck.

"Please help yourselves," Edward said to the children. "Breakfast is very informal here."

The Aldens piled their plates with homemade granola, fruit, Maryland ham, and scrambled eggs.

"Where's Dorsey?" Benny wanted to know.

"Maybe sleeping late," Henry said, pouring his brother a glass of milk. "What should we do first?"

"Let's go explore the rest of the house," suggested Benny.

"Okay, but then we should go back to the attic," Jessie said. "We need to check it out."

Violet nodded. "Maybe we'll find some clues."

"What are we looking for?" Benny asked.

Jessie shrugged. "I hope we'll know when we see it."

The children were finishing their juice when Dorsey came in, yawning. Instead of speaking, he spooned sliced bananas and granola into a bowl. Then he went out on the deck.

"Would you like to show the Aldens around the house?" Edward asked Dorsey.

"Not really." The boy stared glumly at the bay.

Edward and Grandfather came inside. Violet could see the disappointment in Mr. Singleton's eyes. She wondered why Dorsey was so rude to his great-uncle.

"Can we see your stuff now?" Benny asked eagerly.

"Guided tour, this way!" said Edward.

They went upstairs to the second floor, where Edward showed them his bedroom, a sitting room, a library, and the room where Melanie was cataloging his collections. That door was closed, but they could hear the *peck-peck* of a typewriter.

Back on the first floor, they looked into Edward's office, the parlor across from it, and several rooms displaying his collections.

They viewed cases of prizes won at early carnivals, models of Ferris wheels and merry-go-rounds, a real Wheel of Fortune game, a Guess-Your-Weight machine, and a band organ. Edward turned a crank. The nickel-plated pipes began to tootle "Dixie."

"This was a popular tune around the turn of the century," Edward said as the music tinkled away.

Most of the collections were small items, displayed in glass-fronted cabinets. Jessie bent down to study one case. She lost count of the vases, pennants, tops, dolls, tin mugs, advertising buttons, darning eggs, matchboxes, shoehorns, and harmonicas arranged on a single jam-packed shelf.

"Now you see why I need Melanie to catalog my things," Edward said, smiling.

They had arrived in the first-floor entryway. A huge carved cabinet stood opposite the stained-glass window over the front door. The cabinet was so big, it covered the entire wall.

Benny noticed a large carved tiger statue on top. The tiger bared its fangs in a silent roar.

"I didn't see that before," he said.

"The tiger and the cabinet have always been in that spot," Edward told him. "My father said the captain bought these pieces, but he didn't know from where."

Benny couldn't take his eyes off the tiger. Triangles of red and blue light from the window made the tiger look mysterious. The animal's glass eyes seemed to follow him.

Weird, he thought. Maybe Dorsey was

right. Cliffwalk Manor *was* a strange house.

The tour over, the Aldens were free to explore the attic.

This time the fun-house mirror made them laugh as they passed it on the fourth-floor landing.

The attic was vast, with rooms and cubbyholes filled with cast-off furnishings and boxes.

"Let's go into this room first," said Henry, turning into a doorway.

Inside, a figure was hunched over a box. Suddenly the figure jumped up, dropping the contents of the box.

"Oh! It's you," cried Melanie Preston. "You scared me."

"Sorry," Jessie apologized. "We didn't know anyone was up here. We thought we heard you typing in your office."

"I was, but . . . then I came up here."

"We'll pick these up," Henry offered. Kneeling, he began scooping old postcards into a pile. "These look interesting."

"I'm working on the last of Mr. Singleton's collections," Melanie said. "He must have thousands of postcards. These are all from the St. Louis World's Fair of 1904."

With everyone helping, the scattered cards were soon back in the cardboard box. Melanie immediately took the box downstairs to her workroom on the second floor.

"She's sure in a hurry," Benny observed.

"Maybe she has to finish by a certain time," Violet said, looking around. She saw something white under the leg of a table. "Oops. Looks like we missed one."

But it wasn't a postcard. It was a photograph of a man with wavy hair, wearing an old-fashioned suit. The man held a fanned-out deck of cards in his hands.

"What strange eyes," Jessie murmured.

Benny thought so, too. The man's eyes reminded him of something, but he couldn't think what.

"Maybe his name is on the back." Henry flipped the photograph over.

In a fancy script was written, *Harry Houdini*.

Violet gasped. "Harry Houdini! That's the magician who was in this house years ago! He said strange things would happen here."

"Just because we found his photograph doesn't mean he's connected to the things happening lately," Henry said reasonably.

"Mr. Singleton has a big library," Jessie remembered from their tour. "He said we could use the books in there. Let's see if we can find anything about Harry Houdini."

The library was on the second floor next to Melanie's workroom. Her door was closed again, but the library was open.

As the Aldens scanned the bookshelves, Dorsey Pindar wandered in.

"What are you doing in my great-uncle's library?" he demanded.

"We found a picture of Harry Houdini in the attic," Violet replied. "We're trying to find a book about him."

"Here's one!" Jessie pulled a thick volume from the shelf. She opened the book on the library table as everyone gathered around. Then she began to read.

They learned that at the beginning of his career, Harry Houdini and various partners played in small places with other entertainment acts, like a strong man. Harry worked for "throw money," passing around a hat after his performance.

By 1893, Harry Houdini had started calling himself the Handcuff King and Escape Artist. One of his tricks involved Houdini being tied in a flannel sack and padlocked in a trunk. The trunk was put into a cabinet by Houdini's assistant, who would step inside, too.

Then a curtain was drawn across the cabinet. Almost instantly the curtain would open again, revealing not the assistant standing there, but Houdini himself. He would unlock the trunk, which now held his assistant inside!

"Wow!" said Benny, when Jessie finished reading. "What a neat guy. I want to be a magician!"

"He does sound cool," Dorsey agreed. Violet had noticed that Dorsey had listened intently as Jessie read about Harry Houdini. He was obviously interested.

"Let's take the photograph and this book

to our rooms," said Violet. "We can read more about Harry Houdini later."

Dorsey followed the Aldens upstairs to the third floor. He stopped when he saw a man in a blue uniform lifting his trunk onto a dolly.

"What are you doing?" he demanded.

"I'm with Express Service," said the man. "I'm supposed to deliver this trunk to Green Acres School in Virginia."

"Oh." Dorsey stood aside and let the man wheel his trunk away. His expression became sullen again.

Jessie held up the book. "Do you want to come learn more about Harry Houdini?"

"No," Dorsey said flatly. "I don't care about some old magician. I can't wait to get out of this weird house."

"This house isn't weird," Henry argued. "It's really pretty neat. Why don't you want to stay here?"

For an answer, Dorsey gave them a glowering look, then went into his room and slammed the door.

CHAPTER 4

The Surprise in the Bread Basket

The next morning was sunny but cool. Edward cooked a pot of hot oatmeal and set out an array of toppings — fresh fruit, brown sugar, honey, raisins, and walnuts.

Benny held up his heaping bowl. "I made an oatmeal sundae!"

"Only you could turn breakfast into dessert," said Henry.

Everyone joined in the laughter, except Dorsey. He slouched at the table, morosely stirring honey into his cereal. While everyone else chattered, he ate in gloomy silence.

"It's such a nice day," Edward said brightly. "Let's go into town. You haven't seen Heron's Bay yet."

"Sounds like fun," Grandfather said. "Let's wash up the dishes and we'll be on our way."

When they were ready, the Aldens climbed into Grandfather's minivan.

"Where's Dorsey?" Violet asked. "Isn't he coming?"

In the front seat, Edward fastened his seat belt. "He said he'd rather stay home. Melanie is there, so he won't be alone."

Violet exchanged a glance with Jessie, who was sitting next to her. They only had a few days to solve the mystery. But even if they solved it, would Dorsey want to live with his great-uncle? It didn't seem likely.

Grandfather steered the minivan down the steep driveway and onto the road that led to Heron's Bay. They drove into the village, which was spread along the Chesapeake. Neat cottages and white-painted churches sparkled in the bright sunshine. Grandfather parked by the harbor.

They strolled along the waterfront. High on a bluff overlooking the town were several redbrick buildings.

"That's the college where Melanie goes," Edward said.

Ambling past little shops that were once homes, the Aldens looked in the windows. One store sold candles. Everything Sailboats sold things for boat collectors.

Violet giggled at the next shop. " 'Paws and Claws,' " she said. "What a cute name for a pet store!"

In the window, bunnies slept or hopped.

"Here's Iona's shop," said Edward, stopping in front of a little white house next to Paws and Claws.

Purple and yellow fall flowers spilled from window boxes. Pumpkins perched on porch steps. A hand-painted sign proclaimed, BAYSIDE TREASURES.

"May we go in?" asked Henry.

"Please do," said Edward. "It's a little tight inside, so your grandfather and I will sit out here on the bench."

Iona Levitt was working behind the

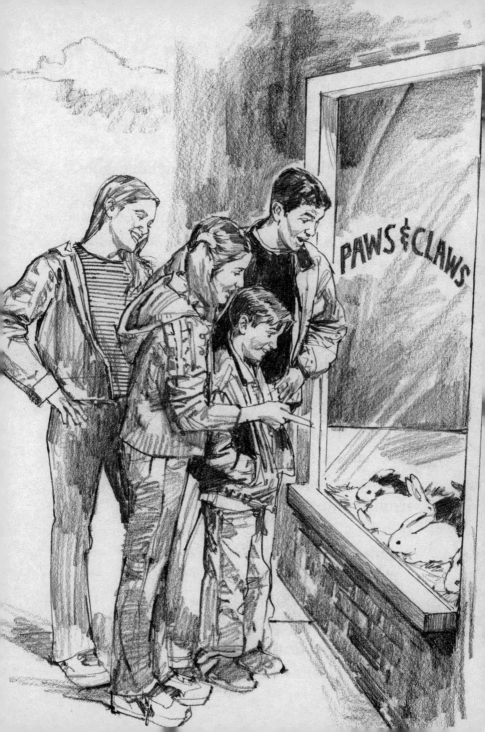

counter. When she saw the Aldens, she glanced up and smiled.

"Hi there!" she greeted. "Welcome to Bayside Treasures. Feel free to browse."

Jessie thought she had seen a lot of knick-knacks and collections at Cliffwalk Manor. Iona's tiny shop appeared to have as much stuff as Mr. Singleton's entire house!

There were boxes made of seashells, rainbow-striped pencils, tinkling wind chimes, hand-painted flowerpots, patchwork pillows, duck decoys, and pale green glass globes suspended in a string net.

"Those are called witch balls," Iona said, noticing Jessie's curiosity. "Actually, they are floats — used by fishermen to keep their nets from sinking."

"Is this a magic store?" Benny asked Iona.

"I think so," she replied. "When people come in here, they always smile. That's magic, don't you think?"

Grandfather had given them some money to spend on souvenirs. Jessie bought one of the witch balls. Violet chose a miniature pewter fairy. Henry selected a brass kaleidoscope for him and Benny to share.

While Iona was writing up their receipt, Benny glimpsed a bracelet by the counter. Its gold links were set with odd stones that reminded him of something.

"This old machine!" exclaimed Iona in exasperation. She thumped the buttons of her old-fashioned cash register.

"Is it broken?" asked Henry.

"No, just contrary, like a mule." Iona unscrewed a metal plate that exposed the inner workings. With her screwdriver, she fiddled with some knobs. At last, the machine began working.

"You're pretty handy," Henry observed.

"I've always been good with contraptions," Iona said with a grin. "Thanks for coming in. Tell Edward I'll be there at five this evening. My night to cook dinner."

Out on the sidewalk, the children relayed Iona's message. Talking about dinner made the children realize they were hungry for lunch.

"There's a great café on the next block,"

Edward suggested. "I hope you like crab cakes."

Inside the cheery restaurant, they all ordered crab-cake sandwiches with onion rings.

"How is the investigation going?" Edward asked the children.

"We found a photograph of Harry Houdini," Henry answered. "It was in a box of postcards Melanie was sorting."

"And then we read about him in a book from your library," Jessie said. "He was a great magician!"

Edward nodded. "He predicted he would become world-famous, and he did."

"Could Harry Houdini have done something to Cliffwalk Manor?" Violet wondered.

"He said he left something behind that night at the party," Edward reminded them. "But nobody knows what it was."

"Maybe he put a magic spell on your house," said Benny. He was remembering the fairy tales Jessie had read to him.

Grandfather shook his head. "That kind of magic is only in storybooks, Benny. Magicians like Harry Houdini are illusionists."

"What's that?" asked Benny.

"You know the expression 'the hand is quicker than the eye'?" said Henry. "That means magicians do tricks that make you *think* it's real magic. But it's not — all the tricks can be explained. You could even do them yourself!"

After lunch, they walked around the rest of the town, then drove back to Cliffwalk Manor.

"Let's go down to the beach," Jessie suggested. "It's too nice to go inside."

"Great idea," Violet said. "I wonder if Dorsey wants to come with us."

They found Dorsey in his room, tinkering with the box Violet had seen the first night. Tubes and tangled wires lay on the carpet.

"What are you building?" asked Henry.

Dorsey looked up with a scowl. "A radio. I had it working. But then something broke again."

"Do you want to go down to the beach with us?" Violet invited.

"I guess," he replied without enthusiasm. "Nothing else to do around this old place anyway."

Outside, the children took a flight of steps from the back deck down to the beach.

It was too cold to go in the water, but they searched for shells and watched birds skimming over the waves until suppertime.

"Come and get it!" Iona Levitt called from the deck. She had dressed up for supper and was wearing a flowing turquoise caftan with bell-like sleeves.

A tureen of steaming clam chowder waited on the merry-go-round table. Iona brought in a towel-wrapped basket of freshly baked bread.

Melanie joined them, sitting across from Jessie in the swan chariot. Since the swan chariot seated two, Dorsey sat beside her.

"Things seem pretty normal lately," Iona remarked. "Maybe those silly pranks have stopped."

"I certainly hope so," said Edward.

Melanie spoke up. "You don't think

Harry Houdini is making them happen somehow?"

Henry helped himself to a second piece of bread. "We were talking about that at lunch today. Harry Houdini was talented, but he was just an escape artist."

"Yeah," Dorsey agreed. "He couldn't do real magic."

"But Houdini was the best magician ever," Grandfather put in. "I doubt anyone will ever be as great as he was."

At that moment, Melanie dropped the butter dish she was passing to Henry.

"Sorry," she said.

Jessie wondered why Melanie wanted to be an actress. She seemed nervous, always dropping things and speaking so shyly.

"We need more bread," Iona said, picking up the basket. "Why does this feel so heavy?"

She unfolded a corner of the towel, revealing the twitching pink nose of a white baby rabbit!

CHAPTER 5

It Can't Be!

"Oh, boy!" Benny exclaimed. "A bunny!"

Edward stood up, shocked. "Where did that rabbit come from? If this is a joke, it's not funny. Iona, did you put the rabbit in there?"

"Don't be ridiculous!" she snorted.

"Then who did it?"

But Edward's question hung in midair, like a puff of magician's smoke.

"I've heard of pulling a rabbit out of a hat, but never a bread basket!" Iona cuddled the rabbit in her lap.

"He's so cute," said Melanie. "Can I hold him?"

Iona handed the baby rabbit to her. The children gathered around Melanie to pet him.

"What are you going to do with him?" Dorsey asked his great-uncle.

"I guess I'll go into town tomorrow and buy a cage for him," said Edward. "He can stay in a box in the laundry room tonight."

"I'll help Iona with the dishes," said Grandfather, picking up soup bowls. "You kids can fix a place for our new guest."

"I'd better get home," Melanie said, giving the rabbit to Edward. "It's almost dark."

After she left, Edward fetched a large cardboard carton and some clean, soft rags from the basement. He led the children into the laundry room beside the kitchen.

Violet arranged the rags in the bottom of the box. Jessie found two small dishes and filled one with water.

"I'll get some food," Dorsey offered. He came back with chopped carrots and shredded cabbage leaves.

Soon the rabbit was snug in his box, happily chewing on his supper.

"He needs a name," said Violet.

"Houdini," said Benny immediately. "Because he came out of nowhere."

"Good name!" Jessie praised. "But this little guy didn't really come out of nowhere."

"Then how did he get in the bread basket?" Dorsey asked, stroking Houdini's ears.

"Somebody put him there," Henry said firmly. "Maybe it was Iona. She had on that dress with the big sleeves."

Jessie nodded excitedly. "She could have smuggled the rabbit inside those sleeves. And slipped him into the basket when no one was looking."

"Her shop is right next to Paws and Claws," Violet said. "She could have bought one of the bunnies we saw in the window."

"But why would Iona put a rabbit in the basket?" Dorsey questioned. "She's my great-uncle's best friend. It doesn't make sense that she'd pull a prank on him."

"Right now, nothing makes sense," Henry commented.

"Anyway," Dorsey pointed out, "everyone is wearing something kind of loose. We all have on sweaters. Melanie had on a big sweatshirt. Anybody could have smuggled this little guy in."

"True," Violet agreed. She noticed that Dorsey seemed happy about the rabbit. Did *he* buy the rabbit on a trip into town and sneak the animal into the house so he could have a pet?

They played with Houdini until the rabbit fell asleep in a nest of rags.

Iona had gone home. Edward and Grandfather were reading the newspaper in the parlor.

"We named the bunny Houdini," Benny told them.

Edward laughed. "Perfect name for a rabbit that appeared at our table!" He glanced outside the window. "Full moon tonight. There's something I want you to see."

They all went out on the deck in the chilly air. Lights from barges sparkled on the water like fireflies. A huge pumpkin-shaped moon lit a path across the bay.

Benny stuffed his hands in the pockets of his jeans. The cold, dark sky was filled with loud twitterings and calls.

"What is that noise?" he asked.

"Birds," Edward replied. "The Chesapeake Bay is a major migration route for birds flying south every winter. They follow certain paths that are called flyways. This is one of them. Have a look."

He focused the telescope, then helped Benny up on the stool.

Benny stared through the eyepiece. Soon he saw a black mass crossing in front of the yellow moon.

"I see them!" he cried. "Must be a zillion birds!"

"Where are they going?" Violet asked, taking her turn at the telescope.

"Some go to Florida. Some to Mexico," Edward answered. "Some fly as far as South America. It's amazing that they do this every year. They just know where to go."

Dorsey viewed the sight next. "How many birds are in that flock? It seems endless."

"Thousands," his great-uncle replied. "As they fly south, they pick up more bands of birds along the way."

After a few minutes in the frosty air, everyone was ready to go back inside. Edward and Grandfather made hot chocolate, which they served in the parlor.

"That was neat," said Jessie, dunking her marshmallow with her spoon. "I never knew birds were so smart."

"I wonder if the birds think they are going home when they fly south," Dorsey mused. "Or if they think they are leaving home. Where is home for them?"

Violet looked at Dorsey. Maybe he was feeling homeless, too.

Just then the phone rang. Edward got up to answer it.

"Hello," he said. "Yes, this is Mr. Singleton. Yes, I'll make sure Dorsey has the right school supplies. I did receive your list."

Jessie watched Dorsey's face during this conversation. He put down his mug, suddenly looking downcast.

When Edward hung up, Dorsey asked,

"That was the boarding school, wasn't it?"

Edward nodded. "They were just checking on last-minute details. You leave in a few days, you know."

Dorsey jumped up, knocking a cushion to the floor. "And I can't wait to get out of this crazy house!"

He stomped upstairs without saying good night.

"That boy is so moody," Edward said. "He was fine when we were outside watching the birds."

"Maybe he just misses his parents," Grandfather said reassuringly.

Edward nodded. "Or maybe he's just tired after a long day. It's been a long day for all of us. I think we should turn in."

On the way to their rooms, the Alden children paused to discuss the latest events.

"Why do you think Dorsey is acting so strangely?" Henry wanted to know. "Mr. Singleton was right — he was fine out on the deck. He changed when his uncle got that phone call."

"I don't know why he's so anxious to

leave Cliffwalk Manor," Jessie put in. "If I were Dorsey, I'd want to stay."

"Well, we have enough to handle trying to solve this mystery," said Violet. "Who else could have made the rabbit appear in the bread basket besides Iona?"

"Dorsey could have done it," Benny mentioned. "He had on a sweater with big pockets. He could have put the rabbit in one of the pockets."

"Benny's right," said Jessie. "Dorsey didn't go with us today, but he and Melanie could have driven to town. One of them could have bought the rabbit in the pet store next to Iona's shop."

"Actually, Melanie could have gotten the rabbit anytime," said Violet. "Her college is on the hill right above Heron's Bay."

"But why?" Henry asked. "Iona is Edward's good friend and Melanie is working for him. What would either of them gain by causing trouble?"

They had reached Dorsey's bedroom. The door was firmly shut.

"Maybe Dorsey figures he can get away

with pulling pranks," Henry said. "He's good with gadgets. He could be making the fortune-teller move and other stuff."

"That's a good point," Jessie agreed. "I feel kind of sorry for him. It seems like he shuts himself in his room a lot."

"We can't do any more tonight," said Henry.

The boys said good night and went down the hall to their own room.

Before Violet closed their bedroom door, she thought she heard muffled sobs across the hall. But a moment later, music came on and drowned them out.

Down the hall Benny switched off the lamp in the boys' room, then he plumped his pillow and tried to go to sleep. But he kept seeing a light flickering on the opposite wall.

"What is that light?" he asked his brother.

Henry tossed back the quilt. "Let's go see."

Benny followed Henry to the window.

"Down there." Henry pointed to barges on the bay. "I bet those running lights from the barges are reflecting in our room."

Benny wasn't so sure. The light he saw flickered like a candle. Or a flashlight.

They went back to bed.

As Benny drifted to sleep, he thought he heard faint bumps and scrapes like he had their first night in Cliffwalk Manor. But now the noises seemed to be coming from *down*stairs.

When he opened his eyes, it was morning. Golden sunshine dappled the wall where he'd seen flickering lights the night before.

He and Henry dressed and met the girls in the hall.

Downstairs, they heard Grandfather's and Edward's voices. The two men were staring into Edward's office.

"It can't be!" Edward said unbelievingly. "It just can't be!"

CHAPTER 6

The Backward Rooms

"What is it?" asked Jessie, hurrying forward.

"These rooms have been switched!" Edward declared.

"Switched?" Benny was puzzled. "What do you mean?"

Edward swept his arm in a wide gesture. "All the things from my office are now in the parlor across the hall. And everything from the parlor is now in here! Only the heaviest furniture is still where it belongs."

He was right. Knickknacks and tea tables

were in Edward's office. Rugs, pictures, objects, even the chairs had been reversed. A dainty Queen Anne chair looked funny pulled up to his businesslike desk.

In the parlor, Edward's papers were stacked on the grand piano. Files and notebooks sat on the burgundy sofa. Framed documents from Edward's office hung on the rose-sprigged wallpaper.

Dorsey came up behind Benny. "What's going on?"

"The rooms are backward," Benny replied.

"Weird," Dorsey pronounced, shaking his head. "Haven't I said all along this place is weird?"

"Somebody made this happen," his great-uncle said. "Those things didn't walk across the hall."

"Who could have done it?" asked Violet. "We were all in bed last night."

Or were we? she added to herself. Had Dorsey gotten up in the night to switch rooms?

"We don't know the answer to that now,"

Grandfather said reasonably. "Let's have breakfast before we move Edward's things back where they belong."

While they were eating, Iona came into the dining room.

"How did you get in?" Benny asked her. The doorbell hadn't rung. No one had gone to the door.

"Edward keeps a key hidden under a rock in the garden. Today my shop is closed and I thought I'd come by," she said. "Why the long faces?"

"We'll show you," Henry offered.

When Iona saw the "backward rooms," she clucked her tongue.

"I've said it before: This house is too much for Edward." Her eyes showed concern. "He really needs to get rid of this place before anything worse happens."

"Like what?" Henry asked her.

Iona picked up a toy merry-go-round from Edward's file cabinet. "I don't know. But the pranks are getting more serious. It's one thing to find a stray playing card in the kitchen sink. It's quite another to find

someone has moved all your things over-
night."

Jessie had been thinking. "Maybe this is
some sort of a message. Somebody could be
warning Mr. Singleton about something.
But what?"

At that moment, the front door opened.
Melanie came in, fastening her key ring to
the loop on her backpack. When she saw
Iona and the Alden children in the entry,
she looked nervous.

"What's wrong?" she asked, tugging her
braid over one shoulder.

Benny showed her the backward rooms.
Melanie put her hand over her mouth.

"Oh, my!" she gasped.

Jessie noticed Melanie's key ring.

"Do you have a key?" she asked Melanie.

The student nodded. "Mr. Singleton gave
me one. I work from eight to six, five days
a week. He figured I should have my own
key, in case he wasn't here."

Melanie's green eyes were round and in-
nocent behind her glasses. She seemed as
upset as Iona had been over the switched

rooms. Still, Jessie didn't think anyone could be ruled out as a suspect. Not yet anyway.

Everyone pitched in to switch the rooms back. The men and Henry insisted on carrying the heavier items, but Iona protested.

"I can lift," she said. "I do it all the time in my shop."

To prove it, she hefted a case of books with apparent ease. Then she saw a sprinkling of dust on the baseboard. "Honestly. Edward needs someone around to keep this place cleaner."

Henry noticed her strength. Whoever had moved the things the night before had to be strong enough to lift the old-fashioned tables and chairs, which were made of solid wood.

He noticed that Dorsey was fairly strong, too, for his age. Only Melanie seemed frail in her baggy sweatpants and sweatshirt. But she carried many of the small objects.

Trotting across the hall with the toy merry-go-round, Benny felt eyes on his back. He looked up. The carved tiger glared down from its perch on the huge cabinet in the entryway.

Nothing in the entryway had been touched. Of course, the massive cabinet was too heavy to budge and the tiger was too high to reach. But the eyes of the tiger made Benny scurry into the parlor. That thing gave him the creeps!

When the rooms were back to normal, Iona went to the parlor window and looked out.

"The morning fog has burned off. It looks quite nice outside. Let's have a picnic down on the beach."

"Great idea!" Edward agreed.

"I need to get to work," Melanie said, heading to her office on the second floor.

While the children fed Houdini, Iona put together a fast lunch.

Bundled up in windbreakers, everyone climbed down the steps to the beach below. The grown-ups spread a red plaid blanket on the sand, out of the wind.

The children darted among frothy waves. It was too cold to go wading, but they had fun chasing one another. Even Dorsey ran till he was out of breath and his pale cheeks were pink.

Then Dorsey helped his great-uncle and Iona unpack the big wicker hamper.

The Alden kids walked along the beach and discussed the mystery.

"Who do you think switched those rooms?" Violet asked.

"My guess is Iona," said Henry. "She's plenty strong and she knows where Mr. Singleton keeps the key."

"But why would she pull a stunt on her good friend?" Jessie asked.

Henry shrugged. "Maybe to get him to sell Cliffwalk Manor. She says it's too big for him."

"I think Iona likes Mr. Singleton," Violet said.

"Sure, she likes him," Benny said. "They're friends."

Jessie smiled. "Violet means Iona likes Mr. Singleton *a lot*."

"She could even be a little jealous," Violet went on. "You know, because Mr. Sin-

gleton spends so much time with his collections."

"Good thinking," Jessie remarked. "That gives Iona a motive. But it could have been Melanie, too. She has a key. She could have come back last night after we were all in bed and switched the rooms."

"But what is her motive?" Henry argued. "She seems happy enough cataloging Mr. Singleton's collections."

"I think Dorsey did it," stated Benny.

"So do I," Violet said. "Dorsey acts like he can't wait to get away from Cliffwalk Manor. Maybe he's trying to make his great-uncle send him to that school sooner!"

Henry shook his head. "We're no closer to an answer, I'm afraid. Grandfather is waving. Time to eat!"

They raced one another back to the picnic spot. Iona had made thick tuna salad sandwiches. Tortilla chips, bean soup, and rosy pears rounded out the noonday meal.

Edward entertained them by telling corny

knock-knock jokes. Dorsey laughed so hard, he got the hiccups.

Violet wondered if he *really* wanted to go to Green Acres School. He was having such a good time — why would he want to leave?

Later that afternoon, the phone rang. This time Dorsey answered it in his great-uncle's office.

The Aldens were in the parlor across the hall looking at old postcards that Melanie had arranged neatly in albums. Dorsey didn't close the door; they could hear his end of the conversation.

"Yes, operator, I'll accept the call," they heard him say. "Mom? I'm fine. . . . Yeah, all my stuff is at that dumb school. . . . I don't know who my teachers will be. . . . I don't really care."

Then his voice became muffled; he had shut the door.

"He doesn't sound very happy," Jessie remarked.

Violet agreed. "I don't think Dorsey

wants to go to that school, even though he tells us he can't wait."

"But if he wants to stay, why does he act so anxious to leave?" Henry asked.

Violet didn't answer. The postcards had suddenly reminded her of the photograph of Harry Houdini she had found in the attic. She remembered how strange the magician's eyes were. . . . There was something else about that picture. What was it?

That evening at dinner, the large clock on the sideboard struck three.

"It's after six," Grandfather said, checking his watch. "Better set that clock, Edward."

"I did," said Edward. "Just this morning. It's a good clock. It shouldn't keep losing time."

As if the clock had a mind of its own, it chimed four. Melanie got up and stopped the pendulum. "I'll set it after we eat," she said.

Tonight they had steak and baked potatoes. The table was set with orange glassware Edward said was called carnival glass.

Dishes of that type often had been given away as prizes in games like bingo. A set of ruby glass salt and pepper shakers inscribed *1904 St. Louis World's Fair* stood by the steak platter.

"I'll go into town tomorrow and buy Houdini's cage," Edward said.

"Get a nice big one," Dorsey instructed.

Jessie wondered why he cared. He was only going to be living at Cliffwalk Manor a few more days.

Suddenly Benny pointed toward the meat platter and cried, "Look at that!"

Everyone stared in astonishment.

The ruby glass saltshaker was moving across the table!

"Somebody's jiggling the table," Iona said with a frown. She gripped the edge of the table to steady it.

But the saltshaker hopped past the butter dish. No one was moving the table.

"It's magic," Benny breathed.

CHAPTER 7

Houdini's Gift

"There must be a better expla-
nation," Henry declared, scooping up the
saltshaker.

"Looks like magic to me!" Dorsey said.

Henry peered at the bottom of the saltshaker. "See that piece of steel glued to the
bottom? I bet there's a magnet somewhere
under the table."

Violet bent down and examined the underside of the table. Then she held up a
large flat magnet.

"This was on the ledge," she said.

72

"Just as I thought," said Henry. "Somebody moved the big magnet under the table with the saltshaker on top. Their hand would be hidden. No one would ever know what was going on."

"Let me try." Jessie placed the saltshaker on the table. Then she slid the big magnet directly underneath. The magnetized saltshaker jerked along as if it were walking.

"Clever," Grandfather said.

"But it's not magic," said Edward. "Houdini's 'ghost' is going to have to try harder."

"Who did it?" Benny asked.

No one admitted to the prank.

"This has been interesting, but I have to go home," said Iona, rising.

"Come for breakfast tomorrow," Edward invited. "You, too, Melanie. Who knows what entertainment we'll have with our scrambled eggs? Moving fortune-tellers, hopping saltshakers. Anything could happen."

"Edward and I will take care of these," Grandfather said, collecting the plates. "You young people run along."

Dorsey promptly disappeared upstairs. Melanie followed, murmuring something about finishing some filing.

Alone in the dining room, the Alden children discussed the latest development.

"Well, we know how the saltshaker moved," said Jessie. "But we don't know who did it. Whoever it was, was sitting right there!"

"What about the clock?" Violet said. "Do you think that's been rigged, too?"

"Only one way to find out." Henry opened the glass door of the clock and stopped the pendulum. He felt around and finally pulled out a copper wire. "This probably makes the clock stop and start at weird times. No magic here, either."

"Walking saltshakers and haunted clocks," Jessie said. "Who could have done those things?"

"Dorsey likes to tinker with gadgets," Violet mentioned. "He's always working on that radio."

"Don't forget Iona," Henry said. "Remember how she fixed her cash register?"

"What about Melanie?" asked Benny. "She got up at dinner to fix the clock."

"Benny's right," Jessie said. "We don't know much about her except that she works really hard at her job."

"Why don't we talk to her?" Violet suggested. "She might still be here."

They hurried upstairs to the second-floor workroom. Melanie was gone.

"I didn't hear her leave," said Benny. "Her little blue car makes a lot of noise when she starts it."

"She may be in the attic," Jessie said.

The kids ran up to the fourth floor. In the attic, they found Melanie sifting through a box of letters and documents.

She stood up quickly when she saw the Aldens, shifting a big box in her arms.

"I thought I was through with these papers," she said. "But then I discovered this box behind that old trunk."

The box she was juggling on one knee was large and awkward-looking.

"Can we help you carry that downstairs?" Henry offered.

"No, it's okay — " she started to say. Then she changed her mind. "Yes, that would be nice. It's a little heavy."

Henry took one end of the box and Benny took the other. Together, they carried the box to Melanie's workroom.

The kids hadn't been inside Melanie's workroom before. Boxes were stacked everywhere, spilling papers and items that had to be cataloged. Jessie noticed cardboard tubes, nylon fishing line, thumbtacks, and other things. Melanie wasn't a very neat person, considering she was supposed to be organizing Mr. Singleton's collections.

An old-fashioned typewriter sat on a walnut desk. Bookshelves filled with index boxes lined one wall. Each index box had a label on the front, like "World's Fair Architecture" or "Glass Giveaways."

Melanie explained her filing system. "Each one of those bookcases represents a different exposition or world's fair."

Henry noticed a roll of blank cards in the

typewriter. Melanie must have been typing labels when she decided to go into the attic. He could just make out the label in the typewriter, which read, *Illinois, State Fairs*. The *l*'s were wiggly, possibly because the typewriter was old.

"Looks like a lot of work," Jessie said, commenting on the filing system.

"It is," Melanie agreed. She glanced at the clock. "I don't think I'll do any more tonight. I should go home and feed my cat."

She put on her jacket and slipped her black leather backpack over one shoulder, then lingered in the doorway.

"I feel like I've forgotten something," she said. "Oh, well. Guess it's not important."

The Aldens walked her downstairs.

"Bye," said Benny. "See you tomorrow." He waved as she went out the front door. "She acted kind of funny."

"Yes, she did," Jessie agreed. "Like she was in a big hurry all of a sudden."

"Maybe there's something in the attic she didn't want us to see," said Henry. "Let's go back and check."

Upstairs once more, they went into the room where they had found Melanie. A flashlight lay on top of the trunk.

"This is where she said the box was," Jessie said, following Melanie's dusty shoe prints. "Wait a minute."

"What is it?" asked Violet.

Jessie rocked back and forth. "This floorboard is loose." Then she got down on her hands and knees. "See those marks in the dust? Looks like Melanie was trying to pry up the floorboard."

Violet put her small fingers between the boards. "I can lift it right out! I bet Melanie found the board the same way you did, but her fingers were too big to lift it."

The floorboard came up easily, revealing a dark space beneath.

Henry grabbed the flashlight and clicked it on.

"What do you think you're doing?" said a sharp voice behind them.

Startled, the children jumped up.

Dorsey stood in the doorway. "I said, what do you think you're doing up here?

Does my uncle know you're prowling around his house?"

Violet wondered why he was so defensive. Had he followed them into the attic? If Dorsey was pulling the pranks, he would be suspicious, especially if they were getting close to the truth.

"Melanie was up here a little while ago," Jessie replied. "She found a box of papers. We thought there might be more boxes. And then we found this loose floorboard."

"Is there anything in there?" Dorsey asked, curious.

There was.

While Henry shone the light, Benny reached down and pulled out a wooden cigar box. He blew the dust off the lid.

The children gathered around as Benny opened the box.

"Just some old papers," he said, disappointed. He was hoping for a diamond necklace or gold coins, at the very least.

"Melanie will probably want to file these with the rest of the papers she has," Violet said, riffling through the yellowed documents. "We should take this box down to her work — "

She stopped. One sheet in particular caught her eye.

It was a note, handwritten in graceful script.

"What is it?" asked Henry.

Violet pulled the paper out and read it aloud. " 'Please accept this imported cabinet as a gift to the people of Heron's Bay. Also, the hand-carved tiger, which came from the home of an Indian prince. I hope these gifts make up for my rude behavior at the Singleton Reception.' "

"Is that all it says?" Dorsey asked.

"No, there's something written at the bottom," Violet said. " 'P.S. Remember, there is more than meets the eye.' "

"What does that mean?" Jessie wondered. She stared at her sister. "Violet, what's wrong?"

Violet's hands shook as she pointed at the signature beneath the last line.

"It's signed by *Harry Houdini*," she said, awestruck.

CHAPTER 8

Flying Cards

"What a find!" Jessie exclaimed. "With this clue, we know that Harry Houdini was really in this house the night of the party. He even says so."

"And he didn't leave anything behind," Henry pointed out. "He *sent* something — the cabinet and the wooden tiger."

"Strange presents, for an apology," Violet remarked. "I mean, most people would send flowers or something like that. Not a big piece of furniture."

"I guess Harry Houdini wasn't like most

people," Dorsey said. "That's why he was so famous. But what did he mean by that last part? 'There is more than meets the eye'?"

"I don't know," said Jessie. "Maybe it's another clue."

"We should read more about him," Benny suggested. "Where's that book from Mr. Singleton's library?"

"It's in our room," Violet said, leading the way downstairs.

But the book wasn't on the nightstand where she had left it.

"I put it right here," she insisted, looking behind the nightstand and on the floor. "The photograph of Harry Houdini was inside it. Where can it be?"

"Somebody took it!" Benny declared. "I bet it was Harry Houdini's ghost!"

"Benny, we know the tricks are done mechanically, not magically. Remember the magnet moving the saltshaker?" Jessie said sensibly. "Someone probably decided to borrow the book without telling us."

"I know I saw the book the day we went

to Heron's Bay," Violet said, thinking back. "But it could have disappeared later. We've been out a lot, like today when we went on the picnic."

"Anybody could have taken that book," Henry said.

Even Dorsey, he thought. Dorsey had stayed behind the day they went into town, along with Melanie. One of them could have taken it then.

But Dorsey looked as perplexed as the others. If he had stolen the book and the photograph, he was a pretty good actor.

Just then Grandfather came upstairs. "You all are still up? It's pretty late."

"We were just going to bed," Jessie told him. When he left, she turned to the others. "We'll show Mr. Singleton this note in the morning."

Iona and Melanie would be at breakfast, she knew. She wanted to see their faces when the note was revealed.

"Two more days," Dorsey sighed as they walked downstairs. "Only two more days in this crazy house."

Jessie realized that they would be leaving soon, too. *If only Harry Houdini would reveal his secret*, she thought.

Henry woke to the delicious smells of frying sausages and cinnamon rolls.

Benny was up and almost dressed. "Hurry! We might not get any cinnamon rolls!"

Henry laughed. "I doubt that. Mr. Singleton knows what a big appetite you have." But he hurried just the same.

To Henry's surprise, Dorsey was helping his great-uncle set the table. He put a platter of sausages next to a big bowl of lumpy white cereal. Why was Dorsey being so helpful all of a sudden?

"What's this?" Benny asked when Jessie handed him the bowl of lumpy cereal.

"Grits. You eat them with butter and salt," Edward informed him. "It's a southern dish."

"Butter on cereal!" But after one taste, Benny ate it all and asked for seconds.

"No walking saltshakers today," Iona remarked. "And the clock seems to be fixed. Maybe the pranks are finally over."

Henry watched Dorsey across the table. Were the pranks over because he was going to boarding school the next day?

Violet pulled out the old note. "I just remembered! Look what we found!" She passed the note to Edward.

Slipping on reading glasses, he studied the paper carefully. "Amazing! It's actually from Harry Houdini! I'll have the signature verified, but it seems genuine."

Melanie's green eyes grew round. "Houdini? You found a note from him? Where?"

"Under a loose floorboard in the attic," Jessie answered. "It was in a cigar box with some other papers."

"I wonder how the note got there," said Dorsey.

"Maybe Captain Singleton hid the note," Violet suggested.

"Or maybe Houdini himself," said Henry. "I guess we'll never know who hid the box under the floorboard."

"According to this, Harry sent the cabinet and carved tiger to make up for the way he behaved that night at the reception," Edward said. "That's a pretty extravagant gesture. But then, Houdini was an extravagant man."

"Maybe the cabinet is cursed," said Melanie suddenly.

Everyone stopped eating, forks in midair.

"Cursed?" echoed Iona. "What on earth are you talking about?"

"The night of the party Houdini said strange things would happen in the house — *this* house," Melanie went on. "He said he would leave something of himself behind. If he cursed the cabinet, that would be leaving something of himself. He was a powerful magician, after all."

"Nonsense," Edward scoffed. "Houdini's tricks worked because he used mirrors and other devices to fool the eye."

"But you have to admit, a huge piece of furniture and that ferocious-looking tiger are odd presents," Iona said.

Edward nodded. "Yes, that part is still a

mystery." Then he turned to Dorsey. "What would you like to do on your last full day here?"

Dorsey stared at his plate sullenly. "Nothing."

"Of course, we must do something special. Iona will be back this evening. She's cooking your favorite dinner," said his great-uncle.

"Which reminds me," said Iona. "I need to get to the market before I open my shop. See you all later."

"I have to get to work, too," said Melanie, taking her plate into the kitchen.

"Our turn to clean up," Henry offered.

Dorsey scowled. His helpful mood had vanished. "I don't like doing dishes."

"Why?" asked Benny. "It's fun. We can make soapsuds animals."

First the kids fed Houdini. Edward had bought a wire hutch for the rabbit. As Dorsey played with Houdini, his bad mood disappeared once more, Violet noticed.

Next, Jessie filled the copper sink with hot, soapy water, while Violet, Henry, and

Dorsey carried in the dishes. Benny folded the cloth napkins.

Dorsey went out to bring in the last serving platter. As he walked back into the kitchen, he suddenly gave a cry.

A deck of playing cards flew over his head!

Everyone stared as the brick of cards sailed into the kitchen without scattering. Then the cards dropped neatly into a stack on the floor by the refrigerator.

Benny ran over to the cards. "Wow! I've never seen flying cards before!"

Henry picked up the deck and shuffled them. "The cards aren't stuck together. I thought there'd be thread or something around them. But they're loose. Pretty good trick."

"Is it a whole deck?" asked Violet.

Henry quickly glanced through the cards. "No. The jokers are missing!"

"Who did it?" Jessie demanded. "Who could make those cards fly through the air?"

"Only a real magician," Dorsey answered. "And the only magician we know who was in this house was Houdini."

The rest of the day, the Aldens searched for clues about Houdini's gift. But they didn't find anything.

Shortly before dinnertime, they went into the laundry room to feed Houdini. Dorsey was sitting on an old rug, holding the rabbit.

"He's so cute," said Violet. "Don't you wish you could stay here and keep him?"

Dorsey put the rabbit back in his hutch. "He's just a bunny. I bet there are horses at Green Acres School. Horses are way better than rabbits."

Then he walked out.

"Do you think Dorsey made the cards fly through the air?" asked Jessie.

Henry had been wondering the same thing. "He was just outside the kitchen door when it happened. It's possible, I suppose. Maybe Houdini isn't the only magician around here."

"Not you," Benny said to the rabbit. "We mean the other Houdini."

"The rabbit may as well have done it," said Jessie. "We are no closer to finding out

who is pulling these pranks than we were our first day here!"

That night, Iona met the children at the dining room door. She gave them each a small wooden hammer.

"Are we building something?" Benny wanted to know.

"The mallet is your eating utensil," she said. "We're having a Maryland crab feast!"

Edward came out of the kitchen bearing a huge platter of steaming crabs. "Will this be enough for you, Benny?"

"Wow!" was all Benny could say.

The Aldens needed a lesson in eating crabs, Maryland-style. Soon they were all whacking the shells with their mallets and pulling out the sweet white meat, which they dipped in melted butter.

For a long time, no one spoke. Then Dorsey asked, "When are we leaving tomorrow?"

His great-uncle looked sad. "You don't have to be at Green Acres until the evening. We'll leave around three."

Dorsey gave his crab a hard whack. "I'll be ready."

Jessie glanced at Violet. They both wished they'd solved the mystery before Dorsey left. Tomorrow would be too late.

Soon the paper tablecloth was covered with shells and smears of butter.

"Who wants dessert?" Iona asked. "Cherry turnovers with ice cream!"

Melanie got up. "None for me, thanks. I need to get home and feed my dog." She looked at Dorsey. "I'll see you in the morning before you go."

Dorsey simply shrugged.

She left the room. Iona and Edward headed for the kitchen to prepare dessert.

Just then a wheezing sound made everyone whirl toward the beaded curtain in the corner.

The fortune-teller was moving over her crystal ball.

"Who did that?" Edward demanded. "I didn't see anyone put a token in the slot."

"I thought these tricks were over!" Iona said, shaking her head.

After dessert, the grown-ups went into the kitchen to fix their coffee. Dorsey went straight up to his room.

The Aldens were leaving the dining room when Jessie noticed the small white card on the fortune-teller's brass tray. She picked it up.

"What does your fortune say?" Henry asked her.

"It says, 'Better leave if you know what's good for you.' " Jessie looked at her brother with wide eyes. "That's not a fortune. It's a threat!"

CHAPTER 9

Out of Time!

"What does this mean?" Violet questioned. "Who is supposed to leave? Dorsey?"

"I think the threat is meant for us," Jessie announced. "We're the ones trying to figure out who is pulling these pranks."

"Let me see that card," Henry said. Jessie handed it to him. The *l* in the word *leave* was wobbly. He started to point this out, but Violet spoke up.

"You know, we found out that the clock

and the saltshaker were rigged," she said. "I bet Madame ZaZa is, too."

"Let's check it out," Benny said.

But at that moment, Iona came in from the kitchen carrying a silver tray with a coffeepot and cups.

"Why don't you children join us in the parlor," she said. "Edward has many board games for you to play."

The Aldens looked at one another. They couldn't investigate the fortune-teller now.

In the parlor, Jessie pulled out an old-fashioned game with glass marbles. As she set up the board, she wondered if Iona had overheard their conversation. Was Iona deliberately keeping them out of the dining room?

Through the windows, they could see the wind tossing in the treetops.

"What cold, wild weather," Iona said as Grandfather and Edward entered the room. "A good night to stay in."

"I'll light the fire," said Edward, striking a match to the logs in the fireplace. "See how cozy my house is?"

Iona poured coffee into china cups. "Cliff-walk Manor does have a certain charm, even for its size."

"Shouldn't Dorsey be here with us?" asked Grandfather. "It's his last night."

Edward shook his head. "I've tried every-thing to make it pleasant for that boy. But he just doesn't like it here. I can't under-stand why he'd rather go live with strangers than with family."

Violet wondered if Edward had men-tioned this to Dorsey. She had a feeling Dorsey's great-uncle didn't talk to him very much about personal things. Maybe it was because he was so used to living by himself.

Benny was staring out the window. The moon was full and round over the bay. Sud-denly a huge black cloud blotted out the moonlight.

"What is that?" he asked, awestruck.

Edward stared, too. "Those are birds!" he exclaimed. "That has to be the biggest mi-gration I've ever seen! Out on the deck, everybody!"

Throwing on coats, scarves, and sweaters,

everyone hurried through the French doors. Edward adjusted the telescope, but the enormous flock of birds was plainly visible even without the telescope. Their squawks, tweets, and twitterings could be heard over the wind.

"How many birds are there?" Henry asked Edward.

"Could be a million," Edward answered. "They're still flying over. It'll take twenty minutes at least for them to pass. Dorsey should see this."

"I'll go get him," Violet offered.

She rushed back inside and upstairs to the third floor. Dorsey's door was closed, as always. She rapped on it.

"Dorsey?" she called. "Your great-uncle wants you."

The door swung inward. The room was empty.

Violet raced back downstairs and out on the deck.

"He's not in his room," she reported to Edward. "I don't know where he is."

"He can't be far," said Grandfather. "He's

probably in another part of the house."

Everyone went back inside.

"Let's split up to find him," Edward suggested. "You kids look upstairs. We'll search down here."

As the Alden kids dashed up the marble staircase, Benny asked, "Do you think Dorsey ran away?"

"I don't know," said Jessie. "He didn't act very happy at dinner."

First they checked the rooms on the second floor — Edward's sitting room, Melanie's workroom, Edward's bedroom, and the library. No Dorsey.

Next they looked in all the bedrooms on the third floor. Dorsey hadn't returned to his room and he wasn't in any of the others.

"Now where?" asked Violet.

Jessie had a thought. "The attic!"

They raced down the hall and thumped up the wooden stairs to the fourth floor. Henry yanked the light string. The dim light cast looming shadows on the humpbacked trunks and dressmaker dummies.

Jessie opened the door to one of the storage rooms. She saw boxes and furniture but nothing else. She was about to close the door when she heard a sneeze.

"Dorsey?" she asked hesitantly.

A voice spoke from behind a stack of boxes. "What?"

The kids hurried over. Dorsey was sitting on the floor, looking through a carton. Houdini the rabbit hopped among books and papers.

"We've been hunting all over for you," Henry said. "Your great-uncle is worried."

"I've been trying to find Houdini's secret," Dorsey replied. "The magician, not the bunny."

Violet noticed a book and photograph among the papers. "That's the book that was taken from our room! And the photograph I found."

"They were in this box," Dorsey explained. "I saw Melanie carry the box up here before dinner. I wondered what was in it, so I came up to find out."

"Melanie took the book?" Benny said.

"Why? It belongs in Mr. Singleton's library."

Dorsey shrugged. "I don't know. I thought maybe I'd find out more about the cabinet that Houdini sent to this house. I didn't, though."

Violet had been studying the photograph of Harry Houdini. Now she remembered what it was about the picture that had been bothering her.

"He's wearing a ring here," she said, pointing to his hands in the photograph. "But in the pictures in the book, he never has on any jewelry." She flipped through the book, stopping at a section of photographs.

"You're right," said Jessie. "He's pretty young in this photograph. Maybe after he became a famous magician he stopped wearing rings because they got in the way of his magic tricks."

"Good thinking," Henry praised. "He probably didn't want people looking at his hands too closely when he was performing. I read somewhere that magicians talk a lot while they are performing tricks, to distract people from what they are really doing."

"It's called patter," said Dorsey. "I read about it, too. There's a book on magic in Melanie's workroom."

Jessie and Henry exchanged a glance.

"We didn't know Melanie was interested in magic," Jessie said.

"She reads a lot," Dorsey said. "The book is in a bookcase in her room."

"We need to tell your great-uncle we've found you," said Henry. "But we can stop in Melanie's office on the way downstairs and check out this magic book."

To himself, Henry wondered if Dorsey was telling the truth. Dorsey could have taken the book and picture of Houdini and hidden them in the attic.

Melanie's room was as messy as they remembered. Collectibles and papers were piled on the floor, on chairs, on the bookcases. Fishing line, thumbtacks, copper wire, and other small items tumbled from the bottom desk drawer.

Dorsey walked over to a table and picked

up a small red volume. "This is the book I was telling you about."

Violet read the title out loud. "*Magic Tricks in Five Easy Lessons.*"

Henry walked over to the typewriter. The label in the roller read, *Ferris Wheels*. Again, he saw the *l* in *Wheels* was wiggly. Where had he seen those wiggly *l*'s before?

But Benny had made another discovery. "Isn't that Melanie's backpack?" He pointed to a black leather knapsack in the corner.

"Yeah," said Jessie. "She takes it everywhere. Her car keys are still on the key loop." She drew in a breath. "Melanie said she was leaving. But she didn't. Melanie Preston is still in this house . . . somewhere."

"People sure disappear around here a lot," said Benny. "First Dorsey, now Melanie."

"I didn't disappear," Dorsey said defensively, holding Houdini. "I was in the attic."

"But where is Melanie?" asked Henry. "We looked all over the house when we were searching for Dorsey."

"We should tell Mr. Singleton," Jessie said decisively. "He needs to know Dorsey is okay, anyway."

They ran back downstairs. Edward, Grandfather, and Iona were in the laundry room.

"There you are!" Edward said to Dorsey, relieved. "We were worried about you."

"I'm okay," said Dorsey, putting Houdini back in his cage. "I was just . . . looking for something."

"We think Melanie is here someplace," Jessie told Edward. "Her backpack is in her workroom."

"I don't understand," Edward said. "She said she had to go home and feed her dog."

"I thought she had a cat," said Benny. "Yesterday she said she had to go home and feed her cat."

"I bet she doesn't have either one," Henry stated. Now he realized what was bothering him. He pulled out the latest card from Madame ZaZa's booth. "Look at this."

The others gathered around.

"Notice the *l* in *leave*. See how wiggly it

is?" he said. "The labels in Melanie's typewriter have the same wiggly *l*. And this card is brand-new. The others that came out of the fortune-teller are yellowed and brown-edged with age."

"Are you saying Melanie typed this fortune card?" said Edward.

"Let me check out one thing first." Henry went through the kitchen and into the dining room.

Everyone hurried after him.

Henry looked behind the fortune-telling booth. Reaching under, he pulled out a length of nylon fishing line.

"This is connected to the switch in the back," he said. "It runs along the baseboard, but you can't see it because it's clear." On his hands and knees, he followed the line to the swan chariot. The line was thumbtacked to the underside of the seat.

"We found fishing line and copper wire in Melanie's workroom," said Jessie. "We also found a copper wire inside the clock that made it strike at odd times."

Grandfather examined the line under the

chariot seat. "I see. Whoever sits here just gives a little tug and the fortune-teller starts." He pulled the line to demonstrate. Sure enough, Madame ZaZa whirred into action. "Good work, Henry!"

"But who sits in that seat?" asked Edward.

"Melanie does sometimes, but so does Iona and even Dorsey," answered Violet.

"I didn't — " Dorsey began.

At that moment, they all heard a thump.

"Help!" came a muffled voice.

"It's coming from the hall!" Benny exclaimed.

They all rushed into the entryway.

Thump, thump!

"It sounds like someone is in the big cabinet!" declared Violet.

Edward grasped the wooden handles. "It's locked. I always keep it locked." He produced a small brass key from the ring in his pocket.

"Help me!" cried the voice. "Please!"

Edward quickly unlocked the doors and opened them wide.

But the cabinet was empty!

CHAPTER 10

Benny Figures It Out

"Please get me out!" begged the voice.

"The magician's ghost is in there!" Dorsey exclaimed.

"It's not a ghost," Benny said firmly. He looked up at the tiger perched on top. The tiger seemed to be looking back at him. . . .

"Help!" the voice cried.

Benny noticed the interior of the cabinet seemed smaller than the outside. Was there another door at the back of the cabinet? He began feeling along the inside for a latch or switch.

His search was rewarded. Suddenly a panel slid back, revealing a secret compartment.

Melanie Preston stumbled out of the compartment, pale-cheeked and in tears. "Thank you!"

"What were you doing in there?" Edward demanded.

"After the Aldens found Houdini's note, I knew this was one of his special cabinets," she answered. "I figured it had a place for him to hide. I was right."

"Melanie is your secret prankster," Henry told Edward.

Edward stared at her. "Is this true?"

"It's a long story," said Melanie. "May I sit down?"

"I think we all need to sit down," said Iona. "I'll make fresh coffee and some cocoa for the young people."

Soon they were all settled in the parlor with hot drinks and a plate of peanut butter cookies.

After a few sips of Iona's strong coffee, Melanie looked better. She took a deep breath and began talking.

"I take drama classes at school," she said. "But I'm really a magician."

"You've been practicing your tricks in this house," Violet accused. "Trying to fool Mr. Singleton."

"I practice whenever I can," Melanie said defensively. "Practice makes perfect, they say. But not in my case. When I do a card trick, the cards always land somewhere else."

"You made the cards fly in the kitchen!" said Benny.

Melanie nodded. "The flying card trick actually worked that time. I'd never been able to get them to stay together before. The secret is gravity."

"Show us how it works," Henry said.

Melanie drew a deck of cards from her pocket. She held them in her hand with her thumb on top, fingers beneath.

"The jokers are on the top and bottom," she explained. "I press the cards together to get the air out. Watch carefully." She pulled the top and bottom cards back about an inch. Then she threw. The cards flew in a solid block about ten feet, landing in a neat stack as before.

"You're still holding the jokers," Henry observed. "That's why they were missing from the deck we found."

"I know what you're thinking," said Melanie, as if she could read minds as well. "How can anybody as shy and awkward as me ever be an entertainer? But I want lots of friends and people to admire me."

Iona spoke gently. "You don't need to hide behind a magic act. You have friends right here."

"If I were Uncle Edward, I wouldn't be your friend!" Dorsey blurted. "You haven't been very nice, sneaking around playing tricks."

Melanie hung her head. "I know. But I had a reason."

"Please explain," said Edward. "We're listening."

"Last year I did my term paper on Harry

Houdini," she began. "I learned a lot about him. I even found out about how he used to be hired for private parties. Then I found out he and his brother had been in this very house."

"You got a job here," Violet said, "so you could look for whatever Houdini had left behind."

"Yes," said Melanie. "I figured it was a formula for a terrific trick. If I found it, I could be a great magician like Houdini. Maybe even greater."

Edward looked confused. "I gave you free run of my house and all my collections. Why did you play tricks on me? You could have found Houdini's secret and I would never have known."

"I didn't know what I was looking for," Melanie admitted. "It could have been a piece of paper or a magic item — anything. I practiced my tricks here. If I could fool you, I could fool an audience. But I still had to hunt for Houdini's secret."

Benny spoke up. "You sneaked in at night, didn't you? I saw your flashlight outside the other night."

"I used my key to slip in after everyone was in bed," Melanie said. "While I looked, I moved pictures and stuff, so Mr. Singleton would be spooked. I hoped to make him nervous so he wouldn't notice I was almost finished with my job."

"You pushed books out of bookcases — " Iona said.

"And rigged the clock and saltshaker in the dining room," said Jessie.

"Along with the fortune-teller," added Henry. "You used your typewriter to type that last fortune card. I recognized the *l* from the labels in your workroom."

"You moved the mirror the first night we were here," said Violet. "You act like you aren't very strong, but we caught you lifting that heavy box in the attic."

"I work out at the college gym," Melanie confessed. "I'm a lot stronger than I look. Yes, I did all those things."

Edward shook his head. "Why did you pretend to leave tonight?"

"These kids were getting close to the truth," said Melanie. "While you were all looking at the birds on the deck, I came back in the house."

"You believed Houdini's secret was in the carved cabinet," Violet guessed. "How did you get in it?"

Melanie pulled a bent paper clip from her pocket. "Not very magical, I'm afraid, but it worked. I thought there might be a hidden compartment in the cabinet. It was the only place I hadn't looked yet. And I got trapped."

"That was a foolish thing to do," Iona chided. "The doors locked behind you."

"I know," Melanie said glumly. "And I didn't even find Houdini's secret."

Benny bit into his third cookie. "I know what Houdini's secret is." While the others had been talking, he had figured it out.

Everyone stared at him.

"You do?" asked Grandfather, his eyebrows raised.

"Yeah. It's not *in* the cabinet," he said. "It's *on* the cabinet."

"What are you talking about?" Jessie asked her brother.

Benny stood up. "Come in the hall. I'll show you." In front of the cabinet, he pointed to the tiger. "The thing Houdini left behind is on the tiger. But we can't reach."

"I'll get a ladder." Edward was back in a few minutes with a stepladder. He brought the tiger down and set it carefully on the marble floor.

"What did Houdini leave behind?" Grandfather asked Benny.

Benny touched the right eye of the tiger. It popped out in his hand. When he held it up, they could all see the eye was really a gold ring set with an amber-colored stone. The stone had a dark stripe down the center, like the pupil of a cat's eye.

"The ring in the photograph!" Violet exclaimed. "It's the ring Houdini is wearing in that picture we found!"

"I'll get the picture," Jessie offered, racing upstairs. She returned with both the book about Houdini and the photograph.

Melanie couldn't believe it. "I studied that picture, but I never noticed the ring!"

Iona examined the tiger. "The left eye is amber glass. The stone in this ring is tiger's-eye, an actual stone. I have a bracelet in my shop made of tiger's-eye."

Benny nodded. "I saw it when we were in your shop. Every time I came in here, I felt like the tiger was looking at me."

"Is the ring magic?" Dorsey wanted to know.

"There are those who say that tiger's-eye makes its wearer feel confident and independent, but also lonely," said Iona. "Maybe that's why Houdini put his ring in the eye of the tiger."

Edward compared the ring to the one Houdini was wearing in the photograph. "They seem to be identical. Do you think Houdini put his ring in the tiger so everyone in the house would be lonely? Or was it truly a gift?"

"I don't think we'll ever know," said Grandfather. "But the ring is a nice addition for your collection."

"Now, what about you?" Edward asked Melanie. "Do you think I should fire you?"

"I wouldn't blame you if you did," she said sadly. Then she lifted her chin. "But you and Iona are my friends, the closest friends I have. I'd like to finish cataloging your collections, Mr. Singleton, without pay. I'm very sorry for the trouble I caused."

Edward sighed. "Well, I always believe in giving people a second chance. But you'll have to hand over the key to this house."

Gratefully, Melanie surrendered her key. "Thanks for not being mad. You're terrific!" She looked at Dorsey. "Too bad you can't see that."

To everyone's surprise, Dorsey burst into tears.

"I know Uncle Edward is great," he sobbed. "I wish I didn't have to go to that school!"

Edward looked at him in surprise. "But you've acted like you can't wait to leave Cliffwalk Manor."

"I love Cliffwalk Manor," Dorsey sniffed. "It's the neatest house I've ever seen."

Violet spoke up. "I think Dorsey was

afraid to tell you because he thought everyone expected him to go to boarding school. He didn't know how to tell you he wanted to stay here."

"And you didn't tell him you wanted him to stay," Jessie said to Edward. "It's a big misunderstanding."

"I'll say!" said Edward. "Dorsey, of course I want you to live with me. If that's what *you* want. We'll call your parents tonight."

"Can I keep Houdini?" asked Dorsey. "The rabbit, I mean."

His great-uncle laughed. "You bet! And tomorrow we'll send for your things from that school."

"Sounds like Cliffwalk Manor won't be so lonely anymore," said Grandfather.

Edward turned to Iona. "You've been dropping hints about how this house is too much for me."

"Are you planning on moving?" Iona said, her blue eyes twinkling.

Edward smiled. "James is right. A house is not a home without a family. No matter how many things I have, I need more people in my life. A long time ago I asked you to marry me."

"I thought you were kidding," Iona said.

"I wasn't kidding then and I'm not now." Edward held her hand. "Will you marry me, Iona?"

"Yes, Edward, I will marry you," Iona said, hugging him. "And I'll be happy to live in this great big house. Cliffwalk Manor does have a special magic." She turned to Dorsey. "Is this okay with you?"

"You bet!" he said. "You're a better cook anyway!"

"This calls for a celebration!" said James Alden, going into the kitchen.

Soon he produced a bottle of bubbling ginger ale, which he poured into antique glasses. He raised his glass to the ceiling, preparing to give a toast.

"Wait!" cried Dorsey. "We're not all here." He rushed off and came back with Houdini, the rabbit. "Okay, now everybody is here."

"To the family in Cliffwalk Manor," said

Grandfather. "May they find the magic of happiness always."

"Hear, hear!" said Henry.

They all clinked glasses, then sipped the ginger ale.

"How about a toast to the Alden detectives?" said Edward.

"Hear, hear!" Dorsey cheered.

Everyone lifted their glasses once more.

"I have a toast," said Benny. "I hope the next mystery will be as fun as this one!"

"Hear, hear!" chimed Jessie, Henry, and Violet.

A Magic Mansion?

When Grandfather is invited to his friend Edward's mansion in Maryland, the Alden children can hardly wait to visit the scenic area of Chesapeake Bay. But as soon as they arrive at Edward's home, strange and mysterious magic tricks begin to happen right before their eyes!

Could it be the ghost of Harry Houdini, the famous magician who once visited this enormous house? Or is someone else responsible for the magical mayhem? Edward enlists the help of Henry, Jessie, Violet, and Benny to find the answers.

Turn the page to begin testing your own puzzle-solving skills. You can check your answers at the back of the book. Good luck!

Map Fun

Edward Singleton's beautiful mansion is known as Cliffwalk Manor. It's located in the state of Maryland, on the eastern coast of the United States. Use the map below to help you answer clues about Maryland and the surrounding areas. Then fill in the puzzle.

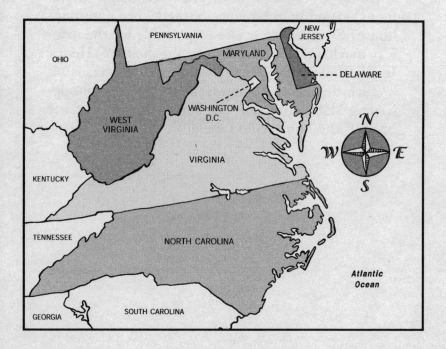

Across

4. This state is south of Virginia.
5. This state borders on eastern Maryland.
6. This state borders on northern North Carolina.

Down

1. This district is home to our president and is *not* a state.
2. This state borders on western Delaware.
3. This state is west of Virginia.

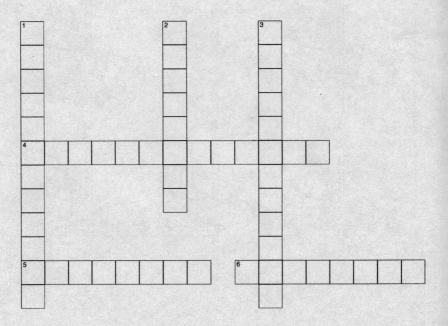

Horsing Around

Cliffwalk Manor is filled with all sorts of souvenirs from historic carnivals and state fairs. There are pennants, tops, harmonicas, mugs, models of Ferris wheels, and even a fortune-telling machine and a real merry-go-round horse!

Take a look at the horses below. Only one of them is an authentic antique from a state fair that took place in the early 1900s. Can you tell which horse it is? It's the only one that's different from the others.

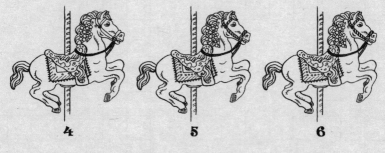

The Hidden Houdini

Henry, Jessie, Violet, and Benny are fascinated by the history of the famous magician Harry Houdini. His incredible magic tricks and daring escapes thrilled audiences around the world in the late nineteenth and early twentieth centuries. Benny wonders whether the strange happenings at Cliffwalk Manor could be the work of Houdini's ghost, up to his old tricks!

Can you find the name HOUDINI in the word search below? It's hidden only once and can be found across, down, diagonal, or backward.

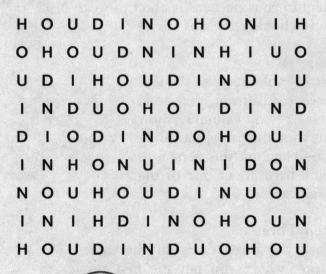

```
H  O  U  D  I  N  O  H  O  N  I  H
O  H  O  U  D  N  I  N  H  I  U  O
U  D  I  H  O  U  D  I  N  D  I  U
I  N  D  U  O  H  O  I  D  I  N  D
D  I  O  D  I  N  D  O  H  O  U  I
I  N  H  O  N  U  I  N  I  D  O  N
N  O  U  H  O  U  D  I  N  U  O  D
I  N  I  H  D  I  N  O  H  O  U  N
H  O  U  D  I  N  D  U  O  H  O  U
```

Harry Houdini

Step Right Up!

The Aldens aren't quite sure how all of the magic tricks in Edward's house are done — or who's doing them! A little detective work leads to some clever answers. Try your own hand at the magic trick below. With practice, you'll amaze your friends and family with your incredible skills.

Step One
Find an ordinary deck of cards. Before your show begins, remove any two cards from the deck and place them in your pocket. (It's best to wear loose clothing for this trick.)

Step Two
Ask a volunteer to choose three cards from the deck. This person should show everyone the cards, including you. Then ask this person to think hard about one of the three cards.

Step Three
Place the three cards in the same pocket where you put the first two cards you chose. Remember the order of the three cards as you place them in your pocket. Put them *in front of* the first two cards, keeping the two you chose earlier closest to your body. This will be very important later!

Step Four

Pull out the two cards that you chose before your show. (You'll know which ones they are without looking because they're closest to your body.) Your audience will think these are two of the three cards you just placed in your pocket. Without looking at the cards or showing them to the audience, place them facedown on a table.

Step Five

Now for the big moment! Ask the volunteer to tell you which card he or she has been thinking of, and that will be the card that is left in your pocket. When the person says which card it is, pull

the correct card from the three in your pocket (you'll know which one it is without looking because you memorized the order of the cards).

Congratulations! You're a magician!

Migration Formation

The deck of Cliffwalk Manor is the perfect place to view the migration of birds flying south for the winter. The Aldens use Edward Singleton's telescope to watch their feathered friends soar across the moon over Chesapeake Bay. Color this picture any way you like. Try to remember all that you see. Then turn the page and test your memory.

Do You Remember?

Test your memory by answering the following questions.

1. Which of the following chairs matches the one on the deck?

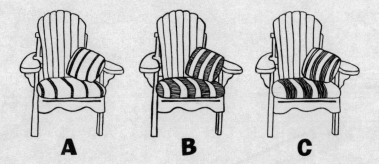

A   **B**   **C**

2. How many birds are flying directly in front of the moon? _____

3. Which side of the deck is the pail on?

_____

4. How many flowers are in the flowerpot?

_____

5. Is the telescope pointing toward the right side or the left side of the bay?

_____

A Message from the Past

When the Aldens find a mysterious box beneath the floorboards of Edward's attic, they think it's filled only with dusty papers and receipts. But then Violet finds something unexpected — a handwritten note from Harry Houdini himself! Help discover the hidden message below by crossing out the letters **Q**, **X**, and **Z**. The remaining letters will spell out Houdini's words.

Z	R	X	Q	E	M	Q	E	X	Z	M	Z	B	X	E	R
Q	T	Z	H	X	Q	E	X	R	Z	E	Q	I	X	Q	S
M	X	O	Q	Z	R	Q	E	X	Q	T	X	H	A	Z	N
Z	M	X	Z	E	Q	E	Z	Q	T	Z	Q	X	S	Q	Z
X	Q	T	X	Z	H	Q	X	E	X	Q	E	Z	Y	X	E

Word Play

With its flying cards, moving furniture, and walking saltshaker, Cliffwalk Manor is a magician's paradise. Henry, Jessie, Violet, and Benny have to use all of their detective skills to find out who's behind the trickery at this mansion. Use your own skills to create three- and four-letter words using the letters in CLIFFWALK MANOR. Twenty is good, thirty is great, and forty is magically magnificent!

CLIFFWALK MANOR

Can You Be a Detective?

The Alden kids make good detectives because they always try to notice even the smallest detail. Think about the mystery you just read and consider the questions below. Try to answer all of them — without peeking back at the story!

1. Which one of the following messages did *not* come out of Madame ZaZa's fortune-telling machine?
   a. "You are in for a big change."
   b. "You will take many trips."
   c. "You will uncover a secret."
   d. "Better leave if you know what's good for you."

2. What do Dorsey's parents do for a living?
   a. They're paleontologists.
   b. They're psychologists.
   c. They're radiologists.
   d. They're archaeologists.

3. Young Harry Houdini used to collect money in a hat after each performance. What was that money called?
   a. "throw money"
   b. "catch money"
   c. "hat money"
   d. "easy money"

4. By what year did Houdini call himself the Handcuff King and Escape Artist?
   a. 1839
   b. 1939
   c. 1893
   d. 1993

5. What is the name of Iona Levitt's shop in Heron's Bay?
   a. Paws and Claws
   b. Bayside Treasures
   c. Knicks and Knacks
   d. Seaside Statues

Answers

Map Fun

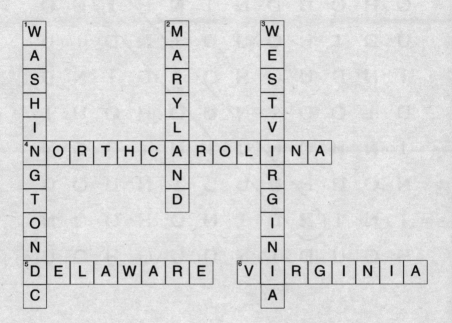

Horsing Around

Horse number four is the correct answer.

The Hidden Houdini

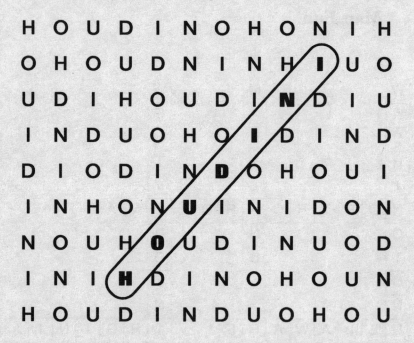

H O U D I N O H O N I H
O H O U D N I N H I U O
U D I H O U D I N D I U
I N D U O H O I D I N D
D I O D I N D O H O U I
I N H O N U I N I D O N
N O U H O U D I N U O D
I N I H D I N O H O U N
H O U D I N D U O H O U

Do You Remember?

1. B
2. Three
3. The right side
4. Four
5. The left side

A Message from the Past

"Remember there is more than meets the eye."

Word Play

Possible words include:
aim, call, can, car, clam, clan, claw, con, cork, fail, fall, fan, far, fill, fir, flaw, for, fork, kill, kin, lack, law, lick, link, mail, main, mall, man, mark, mink, nail, oar, rack, rain, ran, rink, roam, wail, walk, wall, war, wick, win, wink

Can You Be a Detective?

1. C
2. D
3. A
4. C
5. B

GERTRUDE CHANDLER WARNER discovered when she was teaching that many readers who like an exciting story could find no books that were both easy and fun to read. She decided to try to meet this need, and her first book, *The Boxcar Children*, quickly proved she had succeeded.

Miss Warner drew on her own experiences to write the mystery. As a child she spent hours watching trains go by on the tracks opposite her family home. She often dreamed about what it would be like to set up housekeeping in a caboose or freight car — the situation the Alden children find themselves in.

When Miss Warner received requests for more adventures involving Henry, Jessie, Violet, and Benny Alden, she began additional stories. In each, she chose a special setting and introduced unusual or eccentric characters who liked the unpredictable.

While the mystery element is central to each of Miss Warner's books, she never thought of them as strictly juvenile mysteries. She liked to stress the Aldens' independence and resourcefulness and their solid New England devotion to using up and making do. The Aldens go about most of their adventures with as little adult supervision as possible — something else that delights young readers.

Miss Warner lived in Putnam, Connecticut, until her death in 1979. During her lifetime, she received hundreds of letters from girls and boys telling her how much they liked her books.